The Railway Children

Illustrated by Alan Marks

Retold by Susanna Davidson
Based on a story by E. Nesbit

Bobbie, Peter and Phyllis had everything they wanted —
pretty clothes, heaps of toys
and a loving Mother and Father.

Then, on Peter's eighth birthday,
the trouble began.

After the birthday tea, the doorbell rang, sharply.
Three men came in and took Father away with them.

"Where's he gone?" asked Peter.
"He hasn't packed any clothes."

"He had to go quickly — on business,"
said Mother, her eyes bright with tears.

After that,
everything changed.

All the furniture was sold.
The servants left.
Mother was hardly ever at home.

"We have to play at being poor for a while," she said. "We're going to live in the countryside."

They arrived at the new house, late at night. "Let's explore tomorrow," said Peter.

Early the next morning they raced outside, through the garden, down the hill, until they came to a railway track.

There was a great rumbling sound and with a WHOOSH, a train shot out of the tunnel.

It's like a dragon!

"Perhaps it's going to London," yelled Phyllis, above the noise.

"Maybe that's where Father is," said Bobbie.
"If it's a magic train, it'll take our love to him. Let's wave."

Out of a first class carriage window,
an old gentleman waved back.

Every day after that, the children ran down to
the railway to wave to the old gentleman,
and to send their love to Father.

"Let's do something different," Peter suggested one day.
"We could walk along the path by the track."

But when they reached the path,
they heard a strange rumbling noise.

The trees on the bank started sliding downhill,
then fell onto the railway track
with a deafening roar.

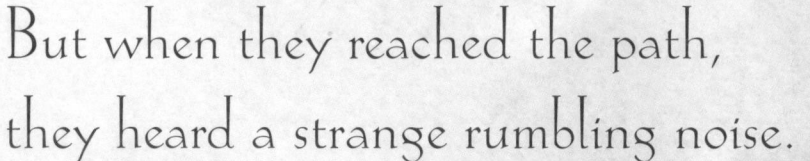

"Oh!" cried Peter. "The 11:29 train will be along any minute. There'll be a terrible accident. We must do something."

"Our red petticoats!" Bobbie exclaimed. "Red is for danger! Let's tear them up and use them as flags."

The train thundered closer. The others sprang out of the way, but Bobbie didn't move. She knew it was dangerous, but she had to make it stop.

With a squeal of brakes the train shuddered to a halt.
"What's going on?" cried the driver.
Peter pointed to the landslide.

The driver gasped in shock. "You children saved lives today," he said.

The Railway Company held a celebration for the children to thank them, with a brass band, bunting and cake.

The Railway Director gave them each a gold watch,
but best of all, their own old gentleman was there.

"Do come back for tea," said Phyllis.

At home, Bobbie took the old gentleman's coat.
She glanced at his newspaper, then stopped and stared.
There was a photograph of Father.

"SPY TRIAL!"
it said.
Then:
"GUILTY"
and
"FIVE YEARS
IN JAIL."

"Oh Daddy!" she cried. "You didn't do it."
Bobbie ran to her room to hide her tears.

"Mother didn't want us to know," she realized.
"She didn't want to worry us."

After tea, when the old gentleman
had gone, Mother came to find
her. Bobbie cried and cried,
but wouldn't say why.

Bobbie was desperate to help.
She decided to write a letter
to the old gentleman.

Dear Friend,

See what it says in this paper.

That is our Father, but he isn't a spy.

Could you find out who did it,

and then they would let Father out of prison.

Just think if it was your Daddy,

how would you feel? Please help me.

Love from,

Bobbie

Time passed, and nothing happened.
Bobbie missed Father so badly,
her mind was filled with wanting him.

Then, one late summer's day,
Bobbie found herself walking to the station, as if in a dream.

She arrived just as a train pulled into the platform.
Only three people got out. An old woman,
the grocer's wife and the third...

"Oh! My Daddy,
my Daddy!"
Bobbie's cry pierced
the air.

"I can't believe you're really here," said Bobbie,
as they walked up the hill together.

"Didn't Mother get my letter?" Father asked.
"They found the real spy. Your old friend helped catch him."

"Now run ahead," he said, "and tell everyone I'm back."

He came up the garden path,
his heart beating fast.
Mother, Bobbie, Peter and Phyllis
stood in the doorway.

"You're home!" they all cried.
"You're home at last."

Taken from an adaptation by Mary Sebag-Montefiore

Edited by Jenny Tyler and Lesley Sims

Designed by Katarina Dragoslavic

This edition published in 2011. First published in 2007 by Usborne Publishing Ltd, 83-85 Saffron Hill, London EC1N 8RT, England.
www.usborne.com Copyright © 2011, 2007 Usborne Publishing Ltd. The name Usborne and the devices 🔔 🎈 are Trade Marks
of Usborne Publishing Ltd. All rights reserved. No part of this publication may be reproduced, stored in a retrieval system,
or transmitted in any form or by any means, electronic, mechanical, photocopying, recording or otherwise,
without the prior permission of the publisher. First published in America in 2011. UE.